Published by Tate Publishing & Enterprises, LLC
127 E. Trade Center Terrace | Mustang, Oklahoma 73064 USA
1.888.361.9473 | www.tatepublishing.com

Tate Publishing is committed to excellence in the publishing industry. The company reflects the philosophy established by the founders, based on Psalm 68:11,
"The Lord gave the word and great was the company of those who published it."

Book design copyright © 2014 by Tate Publishing, LLC. All rights reserved.
Cover and interior design by Rhezette Fiel
Illustrations by Dindo Contento

Published in the United States of America

ISBN: 978-1-63063-364-6
1. Juvenile Fiction / Social Issues / Bullying
2. Juvenile Fiction / Social Issues / Violence
13.12.18

Mic the Monk was wearing his new hat to school. His cousin, Camo Joe, was riding the bus with him today. They were excited to be in the same school together for the first time. Camo was a couple years younger than Mic but they still had tons of fun together.

Camo looked up to his cousin and talked with him about all kinds of things going on in his life. Mic looked out for Camo when other guys wanted to pick on him because he was smaller than a lot of other boys his age.

Later that day, they met at the big slide on the playground. Camo jumped up from slipping down the slide and almost bumped into another boy. Of course, it had to be Big Red, the bully of the school. He had lots of red, curly hair that always seemed to be out of control. Staying back a couple of grades made him larger than anyone else on the playground.

Big Red shouted, "Stay out of my way you wimp!" Then he moved in close and looked like he wanted to punch little Camo.

Mic the Monk stepped up and said, "Hey Red, why don't you meet me after school today and we can settle this then!"

Red yelled, "Okay, Monkey face," trying to agitate Mic more. "I'll be there and you had better be there too!"

Mic just smiled and walked off with Camo close behind. Camo worried all the rest of the day about what would happen. How in the world would Mic be able to take Big Red? He was known all over school for his skill in beating people up. Now, Camo knew that Mic was tough but was he tough enough?

Well, it finally came, the end of a very long day. Camo just decided that he would go and apologize to Big Red and maybe he might let the whole thing drop. He started out of his classroom door and suddenly, there was Big Red.

He stuttered, "B-b-big R-r-red, I'm so...," but Big Red just got up close in his face and whispered, "See ya soon baby face."

Camo Joe almost lost his lunch. Good thing he didn't have the chili dogs or he would have. He looked around quickly for Mic and found him coming down the hall toward him.

"Mic, I ah, just ran into Big Red and tried to apologize but he said, 'See ya soon baby face!'"

Mic smiled at Camo, patted him on the back than started walking toward the exit. Big Red stood outside by the door. Mic got that cute little smirk and told Big Red that they were going to handle this situation like they did in the Old West.

Red looked puzzled. Mic said, "Don't worry, we won't be using guns or swords but pens! After all, I'm sure you have heard that saying, 'The pen is mightier than the sword.'

EXIT

"So Red, get your best pen and meet me by the big oak tree in the middle of the playground."

"Wait a minute!" Big shouted, "What are the rules, who is the judge, and what if I don't want to?"

"Well, if you don't want to," Mic shrugged, "Than I will spread the word that you were chicken. CLUCK, CLUCK, CLUCK!"

"NO!" screamed Big, "Let's get started."

Mic slowly pulls out a small piece of paper from under his hat.

"These are the rules for the poetry contest," he says smiling.

RULES FOR THE POETRY CONTEST

1. We both have to write a 12 line poem that rhymes. You tell why you want to beat me, I tell why you shouldn't.
2. Mr. Slnger, the science teacher is the judge.
3. Thirty minutes is all the time you get.

Red started to tremble because his fingers were nimble but not his brain. His fists and fighting were all he knew and sometimes that was such a strain. His true friends were few and far between, it was hard at times to be so mean.

The timer went off and started to tick but this didn't seem to bother the Mic. He tapped his pencil on his head, then started writing so fast, he almost broke his lead.

REASONS NOT TO BEAT ME UP

I'm cute, I'm funny, I'm somebody's
honey.
I'm smart, good looking, too nice to be
booking,
All over the school, running from you.
So please, Big Red
Don't think I'm too scared,
To confront you with brains,
Instead of your games.
I'm tired of your mouth, your big red hair,
You scaring everyone from here to there.
So put up or shut up
And see how it's done,
When someone else ruins your fun!

Red was stumped, he only had two
lines when the timer went off and he ran
out of time.

Mr. Singer read Mic's poem with great
aplomb and told Mic his poetry was really
the bomb!

Everyone cheered and Red ran away,
not fighting anymore to this very day.

So if you are in a jam or a bind,
Don't forget to use your mind!
It is always good to have something
under your hat.

e|LIVE

listen|imagine|view|experience

AUDIO BOOK DOWNLOAD INCLUDED WITH THIS BOOK!

In your hands you hold a complete digital entertainment package. In addition to the paper version, you receive a free download of the audio version of this book. Simply use the code listed below when visiting our website. Once downloaded to your computer, you can listen to the book through your computer's speakers, burn it to an audio CD or save the file to your portable music device (such as Apple's popular iPod) and listen on the go!

How to get your free audio book digital download:

1. Visit www.tatepublishing.com and click on the e|LIVE logo on the home page.
2. Enter the following coupon code:
   21bb-3568-df98-d4fd-0087-56b2-722a-f77b
3. Download the audio book from your e|LIVE digital locker and begin enjoying your new digital entertainment package today!